Hummingbird Season

Hummingbird Season

STEPHANIE V.W. LUCIANOVIC

BLOOMSBURY
CHILDREN'S BOOKS
NEW YORK   LONDON   OXFORD   NEW DELHI   SYDNEY

BLOOMSBURY CHILDREN'S BOOKS
Bloomsbury Publishing Inc., part of Bloomsbury Publishing Plc
1385 Broadway, New York, NY 10018

BLOOMSBURY, BLOOMSBURY CHILDREN'S BOOKS,
and the Diana logo are trademarks of Bloomsbury Publishing Plc

First published in the United States of America in February 2024
by Bloomsbury Children's Books
www.bloomsbury.com

Bloomsbury books may be purchased for business or promotional use.
For information on bulk purchases please contact Macmillan Corporate and
Premium Sales Department at specialmarkets@macmillan.com

Library of Congress Cataloging-in-Publication Data
Names: Lucianovic, Stephanie V.W., author.
Title: Hummingbird season / Stephanie V.W. Lucianovic.
Description: New York : Bloomsbury, 2024.
Summary: At the height of the COVID-19 pandemic, a young boy
named Archie learns about community, genuine connection,
and how not to lose hope.
Identifiers: LCCN 2023039106 (print) | LCCN 2023039107 (e-book)
ISBN 978-1-5476-1274-1 (hardcover) • ISBN 978-1-5476-1275-8 (e-book)
Subjects: CYAC: Novels in verse. | COVID-19 Pandemic, 2020–Fiction. |
Psychic trauma—Fiction. | Adjustment—Fiction. |
LCGFT: Novels in verse.
Classification: LCC PZ7.5.L79 Hu 2024 (print) |
LCC PZ7.5.L79 (e-book) | DDC [Fic]—dc23
LC record available at https://lccn.loc.gov/2023039106
LC e-book record available at https://lccn.loc.gov/2023039107

Book design by Jeanette Levy
Typeset by Westchester Publishing Services
Printed and bound in the U.S.A.
2 4 6 8 10 9 7 5 3 1

To find out more about our authors and books visit
www.bloomsbury.com and sign up for our newsletters.

For all the students, teachers,
and parents of the pandemic.
And for Ms. Mount and all her sunflowers.

Spring

Stories to Tell Each Other

Every
every
every Friday
we go to Café Borrone
for a family dinner.

It's the only night
we're able
to all be
together.

Without school
or work
or homework
or meetings
or schedules
keeping us apart.

We sit outside
when it's warm.

We sit inside
when it's cold.

We bring books
and
puzzles

and
things to draw
and
stories to tell
one another.

Me and my big brother Hank
used to draw things
together.
Taking turns on
paper.
Taking turns with
pens.

We were silly.
We laughed.

My brother used to sit
with us
the whole time.
Now he goes to the bookstore
next door
alone.

He likes being alone.
I don't know why anyone would
like being alone.

My mom says I'll understand
when I'm older.

(But I know I won't.)

He comes back to the table
only when Dad goes to get him and
only because our food comes.

Then he eats fast
doesn't talk much
and as soon as he's done
he leaves again.

I tell jokes
hoping he'll like them
laugh at them
and stay with me
longer.

I comb through my brain
and the only joke I can think of
is one he told me
on a Friday night

forever ago.

That was when I laughed so hard

I cried
(which I had never ever done before
while laughing)
and I had to cover my mouth
full of my food
because of my Table Manners.

But it's harder for me
to make *him* laugh.

I try anyway:

Knock-knock.

Who's there?

Banana.

Banana who?

Knock-knock.

Who's there?

Banana.

Banana who?

Knock-knock.

Who's there?

Banana.

Banana who?

Knock-knock.

Who's there?

Orange.

Orange who?

Orange you glad I didn't say banana again?

Even if he smiles
instead of rolling his eyes
he still leaves again.

Laughing

My mom has these videos that she loves
(and I love them too)
(and Hank pretends he doesn't love them
but he asks for them to be played
again and again so I think he's wrong about
not loving them).
They are videos of me as a baby
in an indoor swing and
in diapers.
(I don't remember any of this
especially the diapers.)
Hank is just standing in front of the swing.
Just standing there.
Not making funny faces
or noises
or telling jokes.
But every time baby-me
swings forward and sees Hank's face
baby-me laughs.
And then I swing back
and don't laugh.

Swing out
Laugh

Swing out
Laugh

I don't remember these videos.
I only remember seeing them
not being them.

All Hank had to do to make me laugh
was just stand there.
Be there
with me.
And then everything was hilarious.

Friday Night Used to Be the Best Night

We ordered only
the most delicious things.

Hot grilled squid
with lemon
(my brother and I like the tentacles).
Gouda and ham stacked
on fat
greasy focaccia.
A messy fish sandwich
dripping with slaw
salty with bacon.

Hot chocolate
Chocolate mousse
Fruit tart
HUGE cookies

I was always so hungry
waiting
and hungry
and waiting.

When the food finally arrived
I was so happy
I sang to it
in my mouth.

You can always tell when Archie's hungry

my mom said.

He hums while he eats.

She fluffruffled the hair
that was on my head then
but is on the patio now.

That was all before.

It Was a Day

That last Friday was not like
all the other Fridays.
That Friday came after a day
we weren't in school.
And we didn't go back to school on Monday.

It was not a holiday.
It was not a teacher work day.
It was not a wildfire smoke day.

It was a day that started everything.

It was also a day that ended everything.

(Not Real) School

When my dad brought home the bag of supplies
from my (real) school that I'd need
to keep having (not real) school at home
I found worksheets and workbooks
colored paper
a glue stick
crayons

and new
thinner
yellow pencils
that my fingers
don't like gripping
and really don't like writing with.

My fingers never liked
the thicker pencils
we had before now.
But they had gotten used to them.
And when you get used to things
it's almost as if you like them.
Or at least
it's just okay.
Normal.

There's also a notebook.

An empty notebook
that I'm supposed to fill
with words and thoughts and feelings
writing with the new
not normal
unused-to
pencils.

My fingers are already tired.

New Crayons

I love new crayons
their smell
their rainbow lineup
all their unbrokenness
all the things they could draw
and color.

Then Hank walks to the kitchen to sharpen
his new colored *pencils*.

Those are his supplies
now that he's in a different school.
A new
older
away-from-me
school.

A school I'll go to someday
but not now.

I don't even care that I'm closer
to turning a double-digits age
than ever before
because suddenly it feels way more important
to be closer to colored pencils
than crayons.

Hank looks at my crayons
and snorts.

It's the kind of noise
that hits me deep
and mad
and makes me glare back
hard and mean as he is.

I stomp my crayons away from him.
He can keep his snorts
to himself
in his nose.

I have a rainbow
in a box
all to myself.

I have a rainbox.

I touch each color
holding them up
to see
how they feel
and listening
to what they want
to say.

Red is loud.
Yelling and blaring and stomping.
Red is stop and hot and too much.

Way too much
for me
sometimes.

Orange is . . .

Orange is.

I don't know what orange is.

Yellow is a hug.
Warm.
And bright.
Keeping you safe
at night.

Green is new things
and things that grow
other things.
Green knows so much
about everything
it giggles.
But only in secret.

Blue is cool
and deep breaths
and feels wet when
I think about it.

Purple is juicy
and sweet
and laughs a lot.
It's my favorite.

I walk
not stomp
to get some paper.
I like to use all the colors
if I can.
(Even if I can't decide
what orange is.)

But today I want to laugh
so I start with
purple.

Workbooks. Worksheets. Work. Work.

Now school is:
no teacher in front of you
no friends next to you

or across from you

or even in the same room with you.

School is workbooks.
Worksheets.

Writing.
Not talking.
Not hearing.

Just working.

Alone.

I miss my teacher.
I miss Ms. Campbell.
Her smile.
Her kindness.
The way she listened
to everyone.

My mom says it will get better.
We'll probably go back to normal in
a few weeks.

Even be back in the classrooms.
Or we'll have *distance learning* on the computer.
But just for
a few weeks.
At least then we might see our teachers
sometimes.

But right now
it's packs of papers
wrenches of writing
all on my own
alone.

Writing. Righting. Fighting.

I hate writing.
The letters I make
with the thin yellow pencils
that are no good for gripping
make my fingers ache.

Just like when I get a headache
from thinking too hard
my fingers get handaches
from writing too hard.

I'd rather write
with pens.

Softer tips
and easy ink
so I don't have to
press hard
to make myself heard
on the page.

Pens glide and flow
and smooth out my words.
Pencils lurch and stutter.
They make my letters ugly.

New Pencils

My mom doesn't want me to use pens.

> *They're too messy. When you make mistakes, you can't erase them.*

I don't want to use pencils.

> *I make more mistakes with pencils. I make less mistakes with pens!*

My mom goes to a drawer in her desk.
She pulls out a long, narrow box.

It's filled with her extra-special
very important pencils.
Her VIPs.
VIPs cost a lot more than other pencils but she gave them
to herself for Christmas.

> *As a treat*

she said.

She said that she loves how it feels to write with them.
That even making a grocery list is more fun
when she uses them to write it.

She selects a silvery gray pencil

with a pink eraser
a tan pencil
with a gray eraser
a pearly white pencil
with a black eraser.

She sticks each one in the electric pencil sharpener.
It *brrrrrr*s
and
grrrrrrrr
iiiinnnndsss
until each one has a
pricking-sharp

p
o
i
n
t

She hands the three
VIPs
to me.

    Try these. You might like them.

They're mine?
They're mine!

I grip the pencils tight against my chest.

(I get stray gray marks on my shirt but I don't even care
because I can just erase them!)

I get a clean piece of paper.
I start to write.
My letters flow smooth
and dark
and silky-velvety-soft.
I don't have to press very hard
or loud
to make myself heard
on the page.

Later Spring

We're Not Going Back

My dad picked up
more school supplies
from the school
I don't go to anymore.

Instead of
inside a building
my classroom is now
inside a tablet.

School is still
mostly worksheets but
sometimes videos.

And Mom ordered
four sets of headphones
so we can all
block one another out.

Mom also got a standing desk
and set it up
at the kitchen table
where we used to sit
and eat
and laugh
together.
Now she stands there

doesn't sit
and works there
alone.

Dad works in their bedroom
and the door is always
closed.

Even for important questions
like what to do when the videos
don't load or if I tear a worksheet
almost on accident.

Hank turned his dresser
into his desk
and I can't go in our room
when he's *in his school day.*
Not even if I forgot
my socks
which Hank says I don't even need
if we're all home.

Always at home.
Always at home.

All ways
at home.

Vocabulary List

Pandemic
Coronavirus
COVID-19
Surgical masks
Shelter in place
Lockdown
Quarantine
Decontaminated
Hand sanitizer
Distance learning

Social distancing

are words

I did not know before.
I know them all now.

Facts about Quarantine:

Our neighbor upstairs
sneezes really loud.

Our neighbor next door
laughs really loud.

My brother down the hall
pees really loud.

Time

In first grade they started teaching us
how to tell time.
We used a big smiling clock
in the classroom.

With red hands
that moved and eyes that rolled with them.

I liked being able to tell time.
I liked *knowing* what time it was
whenever I needed to know.

But I don't really understand time anymore.
A week feels much longer
than it did before.

A day takes
forever to end.

And time feels like it's made of worksheets.
More and more and more and more
worksheets.
But this time doesn't include friends
or gaga ball at recess
or anything normal.

Spring had just started

and then everything stopped.
Not even spring
moved forward.

The seasons got
locked down
outside.

The way we got
locked down inside.

And every day
feels the same
as the day before.

Nothing changes.
Not even time.

I Am Loud to Know I Am Here

I am loud.
I am loud to know
I am here.
My mom tells me
 Shhh and
 Hush and
 Archie you must be quiet! Everything you do is so
 loud!

So I listen to myself.
The talking I do when I play
by myself
keeps me company
since no friends can come over.
And I can't go over to friends.
Because we're all supposed to stay
far away
from one another.

Sometimes I forget
to listen to
myself
and my car crashes
and building explosions
and train derailments
get so loud
my mom leaves

to work with Dad in another room.
So I get louder
and louder
to make sure she can hear me
all the way down the hall
and through the closed bedroom door
to make sure she knows
and I know
that I am here.

Swollen with Feelings

Sometimes it's like angry and sad
come out of nowhere
to keep me company.

My mom says
I have to calm down.

My dad says
I have to stop worrying.

But they don't tell me how
they just say to do it.

Not Hank

They don't tell *Hank*
to calm down
to stop worrying.

Hank doesn't ever worry.
And he rolls his eyes when I do.
And it's not like the friendly happy rolling eyes
of the clock in first grade.
When his eyes roll
he makes me feel worse than I did
already.
He does that a lot.

So all my feelings come out
spilling everywhere
which makes Hank leave the room.

Leaving me alone.

He doesn't want to deal with me
or my feelings.

Because he's fine.
He's fine alone.

He reads alone.

He plays in our room alone.
He goes on bike rides alone.

Alone is something Hank *wants* to be.

Hank says he *loves*
distance learning.

He chats with his friends online.
He laughs with his friends online.

(Even during school when *I* know
and *he* knows he's not supposed to.)

Hank knows how to take pictures of his homework.
Hank knows how to make videos for assignments.
Hank knows how to log in and log out.

Hank knows.

But he doesn't know me.
Not anymore.

Butter and Salt, Brown Sugar and Cinnamon

When things are normal
(which they aren't now)
my mom doesn't bake.
Sometimes she makes cookies
but not very often.
Now she fills the kitchen with
spices hot nuts brown sugar smells
or
butter garlic salt steam
so thick you
could lick
the air
for a taste of it.

She cuts up
and sets out
cinnamon toast bars with brown crackled tops
or
loaves of pull-apart garlic bread
hot to the touch.
And she doesn't care how much we eat
or even when
we eat it.

I'll make more tomorrow

she says.

She is trying to make
this lockdown
delicious.

People Talked Weird Back Then

I never thought it could happen:
we are all tired of watching TV.
There are too many commercials
about the pandemic
and the lockdown
but also too many shows with no social distancing
or masks.

And I don't know which is worse:
one reminds you by saying it out loud
and the other by not.

So Dad puts on an old-fashioned radio show
from before the pandemic
from before even he was born
where they say things like

   Dagnabbit, Riley!

and

   Now you see here, Buster!

and talk in old-timey accents
that no one ever uses anymore.

And while we listen

all four of us bend around the table
and do puzzle after puzzle.

For a little bit
we are fitting
together
and not just because
we're locked down in the same space
but because we're
piecing together
starlight and colors
straight edges and corners
shadow and sun.

Stay Away

Mom and Dad say
I don't know how
to stay away
when I play.

That my asthma
makes it even more
dangerous
for me right now.

So dangerous that
not even my inhaler
would be enough if
I got COVID.

It's more dangerous for
some other people too.

Where COVID could make them so sick
they'd go to the hospital
and maybe go on machines
to help them breathe.

Our neighbor across the street
is a grandma
who can't see her grandchildren.
It's not asthma

but her age
that makes her more likely
to get very sick from COVID
like me.

So she wears rubber gloves to get her own letters and
packages.
She has all of everything she needs delivered
by mail
or friends.

My mom's best friend
has diabetes
and for reasons I don't understand
that means she
like me
could get very very sick.

My brother can go outside
because he's allowed
because he's older.

Because he
doesn't have asthma.
Or anything else that could
make him very sick.

He wears a mask
and tries to stay away

when he plays
with his friends.

His friends don't wear masks.
They don't really try to stay away.
Not from him
or one another.

It's like they don't know that even if
COVID doesn't affect everyone
the same
it still affects everyone.

I watch my brother play.
I see my brother not staying away.

Six feet!

I yell to my mom

They're not social distancing! They're breaking the rules!

She hushes me.
She sends a hard look out the front door.
My brother catches it.
He jumps away from his friends.

Don't tattle on your brother

she tells me.

I want my mom to make Hank come inside.
He has to come inside if he's not following the rules.
If he's not following the rules he has to come inside
with me.

I have been with my brother
for my whole entire life.
But he hasn't been with me
for his whole entire life.

He had other people
other friends
before he had me.
He doesn't need to be with me.
He wants to be with other people.

I have other people
other friends
but he is my first and my best.
I don't think I'm his best.

I don't know what I need.
But I know what I want.
And they feel like the same thing.

Friends That Don't Talk

This week I tried
to see
to play
to talk
with some of my friends.

My mom arranged the playdates
because Hank has his outdoor friends
his face-to-face
mask-to-unmasked
friends.

And I don't have anyone right now.
Not even Hank.

My mom arranged the playdates
to be over computer screens.

But the first one with Liam
got canceled
because his mom
who is a doctor
got called in to the hospital
and couldn't help him sign in when it was time.

And then when me and Yusen got on our computers
we just sat there.
We sat there doing nothing

just
staring staring staring
at each other.

We didn't know what
to say
we didn't know what
to do
when we couldn't be
together
to run and play
to climb and play
to catch and chase and throw and play.
So we sat there staring.

It was strange
like *we* were
strangers
even though we
knew we were
friends.

Today I tried again.
I played video games
with Bruno.
Still over the computer.

Normally my mom doesn't let me play
video games.

Normally my mom doesn't let me have
this much screen time.

Normally.
Nothing is normal now.

But it didn't feel like we were
playing together.
And when Bruno
kept killing me
in the game
and wouldn't stop
I got mad
and left.
Because he wouldn't listen.

I closed the video game window.
I closed the computer.
I walked away without him seeing me walk away.
Just a blip and I'm gone.

And now it feels hard
to be friends again.

Before when
we got mad at each other
at school

we'd fight
go home
sleep
then see each other
at school
the next day.

And it was like
it didn't happen.
We got to start over.

But we don't
see each other
at school now.

We just see
blank screens
looking back at us
with our own faces.

I'm so so so so so so so SO sick
of my own face.

Summer

Summer Vacation Vocabulary

No camp.
No trips.
No beach.
No friends.

"loneliness"

is a word I knew
before
but it wasn't a word I felt

before

Masking My Self

Now I'm allowed to go outside
on my bike
and with my dad.
He has to make sure I keep my mask on.
He has to make sure I'm distanced.
And safe.

Like a baby.

Hank's eyes tell me
when he runs outside
past me and without me.
Without a babysitter.

Parents don't babysit their own kids. They parent them

Dad tells me
when I complain.

*It's a parent's job to make sure their kids make good decisions
and stay safe.*

Dad says he knows I can make good decisions
but that sometimes I need reminders.
That everyone needs reminders sometimes.
Even Hank.

He also says he needs the fresh air
and exercise as much as I do.

I decide to believe him

today.

So we put on our shoes
and our masks and
we go through the park
and to the pond
where I can see the ducks.

A lot of other people are there
needing the fresh air and exercise.

But not enough people wear their
itchy
hot
masks
like I have to.

I worry the ducks won't know me with
my mask
covering the most important part of
my face.
My mouth.
My smile.
My voice.

The ducks can't hear me calling to them.
They quack over my hellos.
They see me and they flap and paddle
away from me.
I scared them.

I see my face in the pond.
It scares me too.
It's not me.
It's me.
It's only half
me.

I Feel You Stepping on Me

Today in the hottest summer sun
my dad cuts my hair.
He uses a

LOUD

buzz
   -uzz
         -uzzing

clipper.

Just like the lady
at the haircutting place.
But he's not as gentle as the lady
at the haircutting place.
He doesn't know as much.
He reads instructions.
His eyebrows bunch like two huge caterpillars.
He holds my head to the side and watches a video.

He knows all the math in the world.
But he doesn't know how to cut my hair.

And outside there's no TV to watch
while he cuts.
No lollipops

that the haircutting lady
at the haircutting place
gives me
to hold in my mouth
to suck bright green sour apples from
and crunch until my teeth
meet the stick.

Outside my dad sends my hair

    floating

         down

             down

down

to the patio stones.

    Ouch!

I say as Hank steps on my
floats of hair.
I'm trying to joke. Get him to laugh with me.
Or at least smile.

    I feel you stepping on me!

He doesn't laugh
instead he tells me

    No you don't. Hair is just dead cells. You can't feel
    anything from it.

Dad says Hank is next.
Hank says he doesn't want a haircut
he's going to keep his hair the way it is.
Longer to be like Dad
instead of short
to be like me.

Hank's hair gets to stay on his head
gets to stay a part of him.

Hank is wrong.
I *can* feel something
when he steps
on my dead hair
piled on the patio stones.

No longer with me.
No longer on my head.
No longer me.

Other Videos I Don't Remember Happening

My mom has other videos she loves to show us.
I'm still a baby in them
but I'm not the one laughing.

Hank is.

I'm not even trying to make him laugh.
I'm just squirming on my back and making weird baby
noises.

Not making funny faces.
Not telling jokes.
Not even talking
at all.

Nothing.

If I tried to make Hank laugh now
by squirming on my back
and making weird noises
he'd tell me to
stop
acting
like
a
baby.

But a tiny
(probably babyish)
part of me
wishes
I still was one.

Buzzing in My Brain

Dad goes inside
with all his hair-clipping tools.

Then Hank goes inside
with all his hair
and I don't follow either of them.

I push my tufts of hair
around the patio
with the tips of my shoes.

My ears fill up with silence
and my head feels echoey
and empty on the inside.
I touch my head.
Without my hair
it feels
even more empty
on the outside.

BZZZZZZZZIIIIP

Something whips by my ears
past my eyes
too fast to see.

The loud buzz
makes me duck
in case it's a huge bee.

(It sounds like an ENORMOUS bee.)

I look up at green leaves
and pink camellias growing
on the side of the house
but I don't see
any bees.

Instead I see the tiniest bird
that I have ever seen.
That the *world* has ever seen!

I call to Hank through our bedroom window
that opens to the patio.
I can see him on his bed.
I forget about the haircutting
and the hair stepping
and the emptiness inside
and out.

> *I just saw the smallest bird ever and it buzzed right
> by me! I thought it was a bee! I think it might be a
> hummingbird. Do you think it could be a hummingbird?*

He doesn't answer.
So I call his name again
and again and again and again.

When he finally does answer
he's not excited like me.

I dunno. Go look it up or something.

I stare at the tiny bird
who is staying in one place
by working very hard
and very fast to do it.

And suddenly with another buzz
it's gone.

Leaving me behind.

Wishing I could follow.

Who Invented Eyebrows?

I look in the mirror
at my new short hair
and
my eyebrows are suddenly
there

suddenly
THERE
decidedly
weird.

I don't look like me
even more
not like me
than the mask doesn't
look like
me.

I laugh at my eyebrows
so there
so suddenly
so straaaaaaange.

Where did you come from?

I ask them.

Who are you talking to?

But it's not my eyebrows answering.
It's my brother asking.

> *Have you ever noticed how weird eyebrows are?*
> *They're just . . . here!*

I tell him.

> *They've always been there. Just under your bangs*

he says.

I know he's right
but I decide he's not.

I decide that my eyebrows appeared
today
just to make me laugh.

Dead Cells of Me

On the tablet
the school let us keep
over the summer
I read about the kinds of birds that live
near us and
some hummingbirds do.
I also read that some birds might use hair
for nests.

Outside again
I pick up handfuls of my dead cells
    my hair
    me
from the patio
and spread them on the
sharp green spears of grass
outside our kitchen window.
Then I peer between the shades
and watch for birds.
I like thinking that
my dead
hair
could give birds a place
to live.

Please Come Back. Stay.

I saw the hummingbird again today!
I wasn't sure I would see it again!
It didn't pick up my hair.
It didn't stay long enough
to do anything
except
beatbeatbeatbeatbeat
its wings
as its body stayed in
one place
and its wings were
all over
the place.
It was a mini second of brown
slicing the air
outside the window
and then it was
gone
like it never
was.

Love Can Be Noisy

I'd like to have a hummingbird
as a pet
as a friend.
Their wings whir
like Liam's cat's
purr.
And it's a noise
so happy
so cozy
so friendly
it's the kind of noise

    that makes me remember

how I felt every time Mom hugged me
when she picked me up after school.

The times Dad wrapped me in a

          warm
               dry
          towel

so I wouldn't s h i v v v v v v e r
after Saturday swimming lessons.

It makes me remember

whispering across the dark room
with Hank
late
late
late
in the night
when we knew
we should be sleeping
but we wanted to talk
until sleep dragged our eyes
and mouths
quiet.

It makes me remember
how things used to be
before they became different
and changed
and strange.

Still-iness

My mom says
when she was pregnant
with me
she called me *Cricket*
because I was always
jumping
always
kicking
moving
rolling
never
still
inside her.

I think she should have called me
Hummingbird
because it's impossible
for me
to
sit still
even when
I
sit still.

Reading with Dad

Because everything
is closed down
          including colleges and universities
          where Dad works
Dad is home a lot more.
And he's not too busy
or
too falling-asleep tired
to read me longer books
at bedtime.
He's reading books
to me
he never read
to himself.

We snuggle on my bed.
Me, under all my covers.
Him, on top of my covers
but under a fuzzy blanket I tuck
around him.

Mom gives us book after book
and after we finish with one
she asks us

     Did you like it?

What did you think when . . . ?
How about that part where . . . ?

I know Mom thinks
Dad doesn't read enough
because she says so.
He's too busy too busy too busy
to read on his own.
    To read for fun.
I think Mom thinks
Dad doesn't read
the books that do good things
to your heart.

The good
    things

    the good
    books

that make you happy
that make you angry
that make you laugh
that make you think
that even make you cry
(but in a way that makes you feel good)
    (which is strange)

that make you feel something other than the same

as yourself
as your always.

Mom is taking care of
Dad's heart and my heart
at the same time.
Taking care of them
with books.

Sometimes
I see my brother
in the hallway
listening
but
pretending
not
to listen.

Like he's too *old*
to *listen* to stories.

He totally doesn't know
that I know
he's there.
Totally pretending but still
totally listening.

I know he's there
but I can pretend too
so I go back to listening to Dad
and let Hank just stand there.

Pretending to be someone
he isn't.

Birthdays Are Stupid

My birthday is tomorrow.

There will be

cake
candles
singing
presents.

There will NOT be

party
friends
even more presents

BIRTHDAY!

Today is my birthday!

My mom put up streamers
crisscrossing the living room
a pink green blue purple web
of crinkled ribbons.

Outside, our magnolia tree
is hung
with long
swinging strings
of paper cupcake cups in every color.
The cupcake cups
are empty of cupcakes
but full of celebration.

My mom makes my favorite food: bacon pizza and fizzy
strawberry juice.
We are spread out on our front lawn
shaded by the plate-size
lemon-scented blossoms above
all of us
eating together below.

Dad juggles
pins
rings

beanbags
the green grass poking
between the toes
of his bare feet.

Just wait.

He winks
sending the
pins
rings
beanbags
higher and higher.

A car drives slowly
into our cul-de-sac
so slowly
that we have to notice it.

It is covered in signs!
Signs that say

HAPPY BIRTHDAY, ARCHIE!

Signs with pictures of
rainbows
and cupcakes
and bowling balls
and happy faces!

My friend Lilu leans
out the window
waving
her eyes
above her mask
smiling
grinning
laughing.

More cars come
with more signs
more friends waving
with masks under
smiling
happy-birthday
eyes.

It wasn't the birthday party
I thought I'd get to have this year.

But it was also the surprise party
I never dreamed could happen
until today.

This Is a Fart Joke

(When you
hold in
a sneeze
because a sneeze
might infect
someone
then that sneeze
needs to
find
a
way
out
and
sometimes
that
way
out
is
your
butt.)

Inside and Laughing

I love to laugh.
Sometimes I laugh at things
I don't actually understand
because when I laugh with my friends
or my brother
or my parents
I don't feel outside of the joke
I am inside the joke with everyone else.
The louder I laugh
the more people hear me
and if they hear me
it means I'm not alone.

Not a Real Summer Vacation

Because it's summer
and there is no school
it should feel like we're on vacation.

But it's a vacation at our house.
In our house.
And we're all together
  just like last year when we went to the beach
  and spent days dipping into tide pools
  and collecting strange rocks
  and spent nights
  around a fire
  eating finger-sticky s'mores
  and laughing
  and planning new things
  for the next day
but we're not planning new things
for the next day.
Every day
everything
is the same boring same.

And even though we're together
stuck inside the house
we're not really *together*-together.
My dad is in his bedroom for work.
My mom is in the kitchen for work.

And I'm in the living room
watching my brother
play outside.

I want us all to be
together-together.
But my dad says we
all need our
own space.

     Especially right now.

My own space
is lonely.

Especially right now.

I don't know
how you can be lonely
when you're stuck
in your house
with a family
who has no
choice but to be
with you
but I know
that's the way it is.

Maybe if we made s'mores

it would feel like more
of us were sticking together
than just our fingers.

Friends Who Can't Talk

My mom takes me for fresh air
and exercise.
She runs behind me
in a mask.
I bike in front of her
in a mask.

We stop to look at the flowers
looping themselves
through the gray wooden fence.

I wonder if any hummingbirds have been
to visit them.
My mom says that hummingbirds
like flowers that have nectar
for them to drink
and these roses don't have nectar.
But maybe the hummingbirds
would come just
to sniff
and say hi.

I wish we had flowers
with nectar in our garden.
But our garden was the landlord's choice
not ours
and if the hummingbirds come to it

they don't stay very long
because there's
nothing
no one
for them there.

All the flowers in the neighborhood
grow together
not far apart.
Clumped close
the daisies weren't told
about social distancing.

And even if the roses
knew
more than the daisies
do
they wouldn't like it.
They would still want you
to stop
and say hi to them.
And you can't smell—
    their sweetness
        their velvet pink
            their petals that fold into hugging
        one another
—from six feet away.

The flowers have friends.

Daisies get
to grow in groups.
And roses get
to twine together.

Do you want to see my friend Cooper?

I call to my mom.

Cooper is a cat I've met
on walks with my dad.
Cooper is my friend.
My mom would like Cooper.

But my mom can't hear me
behind me
and through my mask.

She asks

What? What? I can't hear you!

By the time she can hear me
I'm hot
and mad
and shouting my question at her.

I make a decision:
she doesn't get to meet Cooper today.

More Eyebrows Thoughts

I wonder if eyebrows
know
just how hilarious they are.

Does everyone think eyebrows are hilarious?
Or only me?

My eyebrows know.
They know
I know
they're funny.

They wiggle
and waggle
and scrunch
together.

They jump
up
and
down.

Eyebrows are the
stand-up
(and scrunch-down)
comedians
of the face.

You can't tell a joke
without them.

Together We're All in This Alone

My mom keeps saying

Everyone is going through this. We're all in this together.

The school message board in the empty parking lot says

WE'RE ALL IN THIS TOGETHER.

Signs all over the city say

WE'RE ALL IN THIS TOGETHER.

Even commercials on TV
and chalk drawings
and messages
on the sidewalk
and in windows
say

WE'RE ALL IN THIS TOGETHER.

But I think that's something
grown-ups say
like

You'll understand when you're older.

They want you
to believe it
they want you
to believe
that *they* believe it.

But no one really
believes it.

How can we all be
together
when we've never felt
further apart?

More Signs

On a walk
I see a new sign
on a neighbor's lawn.

How do you SPREAD HOPE?

I ask my dad.
I point at the sign.

You know, making other people feel hopeful

he says.

Okay, but how?

To me spreading hope sounds like
spreading germs
which we're not supposed to do.
But that's all anyone can ever think about now.
A sneeze isn't just a sneeze
no one can cough
without everyone thinking the same thing.

I think a sign like that just keeps reminding everyone of
what is happening to us and why would anyone want to
do that when we'd all like to forget if we could.
What a dumb sign.

My dad doesn't say anything
for a bit.
I wonder if he's thinking
about germs too.

But then he says

> *You have to take the hope in your heart and try to*
> *make other people believe it.*

I put my hand on my heart.
All I feel is my heartbeat.
I don't feel hope there.

> *What if you don't feel any hope?*

I ask.
He sighs.
His face is sad.

> *Then you have to try and find it*

he says.

We walk a bit more.

> *I'm hoping to find hummingbirds*

I say.

His eyes crinkle
above his mask.
It's a tired
only halfway there
smile.

That counts.

—Archie

Fall

First Day of the New (Not Real) School Year

In the morning
there is rushing.
Not as much as before
because we don't have to drive
to (not real) school now.
We walk
to (not real) school now.
Hank walks to his dresser
which is now his desk again.
I walk
down the hall
to the living room
and at the coffee table
near the couch

    (but never ever on the couch because Dad says
couches make you
    slump and
    slouch and almost
    sleep and
    slumping slouching almost sleeping is
    not for learning)

my mom wakes up the tablet
and   taps
    taps
                      swipes

then tries again until she gets it right

and

the screen becomes
my new (not real) school.

All Gone

I hate the tablet
the school loaned me
to be my (not real) school.
It's the same one I had
last spring.
When (not real) school
wasn't supposed to last
this long.
And it's the one I have to have
this fall.
Because (not real) school
is lasting
forever.

My fingers are clumsy on the screen.
I type on the keypad too slowly.
I drag things by mistake.
Suddenly something happens to the internet.
Like a hiccup.
And all my clumsy finger work and slow typing and
mistake dragging
is gone.
All my work is gone.
All my time is gone.
I have to start

```
a    l    l
o    v    e    r
a    g    a    i    n.
```

PE Class

I move my tablet
so I can move
without my tablet.

I click the link that connects me
to the PE teacher's class.

I don't know her.
She's from a different school
but she's teaching a bunch of schools at once
hundreds of students at once
which seems strange.

And she's a stranger
in an orange shirt.

Right away
she starts telling jokes.

She doesn't take roll.
She doesn't give us online behavior rules.
She just tells jokes.

Then she has us play games!
Inside our houses!

Running and jumping and throwing and stopping and
dashing and leaping

(but somehow safely?).

And then she tells more jokes.
And I'm laughing.

Laughing
sweating
and laughing.

And my heart beats hard
and my stomach muscles
are sore from the happiness
of laughing.

Just Because

I take my orange crayon
and fill an entire page
with the color of my PE teacher's shirt.

I don't know why.
It just feels good
to see
all that orange
all there.

Even if I still don't know
what orange is.

I Hum

I think I am just like a hummingbird.
When I'm at my (not real) school desk at home
I am beatbeatbeatbeatbeating my heart
just to stay in one place
when I really want to

    zip

and sh oo o oo ooo m

    and flitdartdive

far away from here.

    Sit still!

my mom says.

    Pay attention!

I don't want to
stay at my desk.

I want to
be in the sky
on the trees.
I want to find all the other hummingbirds

who would be with me
because I am a hummingbird
just like them
and together we could fly
away from distance learning
away from lockdowns
away from masks
to a place
where COVID
couldn't get
any of us.

Muted

Unmute yourself!

my mom says.

She's supposed to be working
at her job
but she comes to check
on me
at (not real) school.

It's a new school year and your teacher and classmates
want to get to know you!
Unmute yourself! Talk!

I don't unmute myself.
I put my head down on my (not actually a desk) desk
instead.

I don't know that (new) teacher.
I don't know any of those (new) other kids.
They're all strangers
and I don't unmute
for strangers.

Pandemic Outbreak Breakout

The (new) teacher (Ms. Peak) puts me in online rooms
with (new) kids.

We're supposed to talk
we're supposed to share
we're supposed to remember what Ms. Peak told us to
talk and share about.

I don't talk.
I don't share.
I don't remember.

The (new) kids (don't) take turns
screaming over one another.

It's loud so loud so much louder than my so loud.

I take off my headphones.
I mute all of them from my ears.

They're called breakout rooms
because I want to break out of them.

Inside My Thoughts

Ms. Peak says that
parentheses are the punctuation
you use when you want to have
an aside.

Which sounds like when a thought
is on the
side of your
other thoughts.

When it's something I want to say
but not say.
Inside parentheses are the things
I don't want to say
out loud
but have to
let out.

So I say it under my breath.
(Can anyone even hear me?)

Parentheses are like whispering.
People can hear you
but also pretend not to hear you.

They are the mute button
of words
unmuted for your eyes.

She Can't See Me

Today I raise my hand *two* ways.
I click the hand on the tablet
and I raise my hand next to my face.

I want to say something.
I have an answer to give.
I really want to *share*.
I want someone to hear me talk.

We're not supposed to unmute
until the teacher tells us it's our turn.

Ms. Peak never tells me to unmute.
Ms. Peak never says it is my turn.
Ms. Peak has so many squares of students
on her screen
she says sometimes she can't see us all.

But we're not supposed to unmute
until the teacher sees us
and tells us it's our turn.

Ms. Peak
doesn't see me
and she moves on.
So I tuck myself away.
I put my hand
under my armpit

near my
beatingbeatingbeating
heart.

I stay muted.
Today
tomorrow
(maybe) forever.

Nothing about Hank Is Muted

All the way down the hall
I can hear how unmuted Hank is.

His teachers call on him
and he answers.

    Great question, Hank!

I hear his teachers say.
Because they can see *him*.
They can hear *him*.

He works with friends
in breakout rooms.

I think they laugh
more than they work.

He bangs
crashes
laughs
around our room
during his PE class.

I can't even think
when he's not on mute.

He's so loud
on his screen.

He's so in *love*
with his screen.

Even when school is over
he stays on his screen
to do homework right away.

He doesn't even try to get out of it.
Like he used to.
He doesn't waste time.
Like he used to.

He does it
is done
and comes
thumping down the hall.

Happy with himself.
Proud of himself.

If there's a button
that's more muted than mute
I pressed it for him.

Brown Boxes in the Mail

There's a small
brown
cardboard
box in the kitchen.

So much mystery
so much excitement
so much hope
is inside that kind of box
whenever it arrives.

It's all over when it's
wiped down
Windex-ed clean of
possible
potential
problem-causing germs
pried opened

and we see that
all the mystery
and excitement
and hope
was over a few bottles
of kitchen cleaner
and rolls of toilet paper.

These are things that I used to think
were boring
because they were everywhere
and we always had enough.
But they are getting harder
and harder to find now
and that's scary.

Essential Means Must-Have

Some stores are running out
of *essentials*.
Of the things we must have.
Supplies.

I used to think
my essentials
my *must-have* supplies were:
-my LEGO sets
-my trains
-my TV shows.

 But that changed to:
-toilet paper
-hand sanitizer
-soap for the handwashing we do while singing songs to
make sure we wash for twenty full
seconds that we need to do to make sure we get our
hands COVID clean.

Dad showed us how to use less
toilet paper.

(Which made me giggle
and my giggles made my brother roll his eyes.
So I stuck out my tongue at him

but only inside my head
so I wouldn't get in trouble.)

Mom learned how to mix up our own
hand sanitizer.

(Which comes out very stinky and sticky
and takes a lot of hand flaps to get it to dry.)

Both Mom and Dad tell us not to waste soap
until we can order more
from the stores.
And when we do
towers of boxes
filled with our essentials are
stacked on our porch
delivered by another essential.

An essential worker
an essential *person*.

Someone who has to go out
    while we have to stay home
and do their job
    so we can stay safe.

We tape a big sign on our front door
with smiley faces
and hearts

flowers
and stars
to thank the essential people
who bring essential deliveries to our porch
doing their sometimes-unsafe job
that keeps us always-safe.

But Hank says they aren't the only essential people
who can't work from home.
Who have to go out and do their job
because they have no other option.

Nurses and doctors
police and firefighters
postal service and grocery-store workers
garbage collectors and cooks.

They try to keep everything running
they try to keep people safe
they try to keep people alive.

They are the must-have people
in our locked-down world.

I don't want to think about
what would happen
if we ran out of them.

Filled with Ideas

Our next-door neighbor has cats.
They sit in the window
and let me wave at them when Dad and I
walk by.

Sometimes they squeeze their eyes at me
(which I think is their way of waving).
Sometimes they're sleeping
(they do a lot of sleeping).
But today both of them crowd right up against the
window
so close their fur smooshes
flat against the glass.

They don't squeeze their eyes at my wave
because they are staring staring staring
at the little brown birds
bobbing and pecking at seeds
in a bird feeder.

That gives me the best idea
the brightest idea
fills me up with
the most hopefulest idea!

I'll make a hummingbird feeder
and then the hummingbirds will come to me.

And I can be like the cats
staring staring staring
right up against the window.

Empty Bottles to Fill

Since Mom ordered a bunch of new
bottles of kitchen cleaner and kitchen soap
and bathroom soap and so many other bottled
things we need to have lots of so we stay safe
by not going to the store so much I ask if I can
have the empty bottles—the no-longer-boring
bottles. I found a photo of hummingbird
feeders online. You hang them in a tree and
fill them up with what looks like water.
Because of course hummingbirds get
thirsty too. I think I can make one
from a cleaned-out plastic bottle.
I KNOW I can make one from a
cleaned-out plastic bottle!
All I'll need is string and
scissors and something
like a straw for the hummingbirds to rest on while they
drink
the water. And then I'll have a
hummingbird
feeder. And then
I'll have
humming-
birds!

No Bottles No Feeders No Hummingbirds

Instead I have Band-Aids on my fingers
from where the scissors poked me.

And bottles
that won't hang the right way in the tree.

And a very bad mood
because I didn't think
about how
when you poke feeding holes
in the bottom of a bottle
and then fill that bottle up with water
all the water

drips

    down

    to

        the ground

    and

        nothing

is

        left

  for
the

   hummingbirds.

Mom doesn't have time to help me.
Dad doesn't have the right tools.
Hank doesn't care what I want.

But . . .

I do have an allowance.

More Brown Boxes in the Mail

This time, my mom wipes the box down
right away.
She doesn't put it aside to decontaminate
for a few days.
She wipes it down because she's going to open it
now.

Because it's going to mean something
now.

Inside are four
small
round
red
yellow
somethings.

They look like flowers
but not.
They look like cups
but not.

My mom says

    Here they are! The feeders you ordered!

Even though I already know

I knew right away
I knew as soon as the box arrived.
It was a box that looked hopeful.

I am no longer muted.
I am loud
and excited
and happy.

My heart is beatbeatbeatbeating
and I am trying to stay
in one place.

But it's very
hard
impossible
not going to happen.

My Hummingbird Journal

To take care of hummingbirds
I'm going to write about hummingbirds.

My mom says that's the best way
to keep track
to remember
to record
what
and when
and how.

And sometimes
why.

I'm going to write careful
and slow
and using my VIPs.

Because I don't want to forget
anything.

Lemonade for Hummingbirds

The first thing to keep track of is: food.

I search the internet
and find a recipe for
hummingbird food
(which is hummingbird *nectar*)
from a national
and important zoo.

They know what they are talking about.

> Recipe to Get Hummingbirds:
>
> 1 part sugar
> 4 parts water
>
> Mix it together.

I ask
> *Is that all we have to do?*

Mom says

> *I know a trick. It's my lemonade trick—we'll make a
> simple syrup.*
> *That helps to dissolve the sugar so it won't be grainy.*

Mom adds

1 cup sugar
4 cups water
to a small pot on the stove.

She swirls them together
over the hot
blue flame
her hand doing a slow dance.

Then she hands
the wooden spoon
to me and I'm

stirring
stirring
stirring

until the sugar
gently
slowly
melts into the water.
Until the water and sugar are not
two
separate
parts
but one
together
nectar.

My mom makes the best

person lemonade
and now we make the best
hummingbird nectar.
Together.

Loaded with Nectar

We make so much nectar
we have to put the extra nectar
in glass jars
in the fridge.

My mom clears
an area on a shelf
just for the jars of nectar.

Two whole jars
with lids I screw on
as tight as I can.

It will feed so many
hummingbirds.

We will feed so many
hummingbirds.

Café Hummingbird

Before we can put the filled feeders out
Mom says we need to clean the windows.

Otherwise the suction cups won't
suck
the glass and stay
stuck
for our flying customers.

With bright blue spray
and a paper towel
I squeak the windows clean.

I wipe away
dust
and dirt
and dead bugs.

You don't need to clean the entire window

my mom says

just a small part of it.

But I want our entire
hummingbird restaurant
to be bright

and clean
and sparkling.

I want the hummingbirds
to feel like I do
at Café Borrone.

I want the hummingbirds to
feel at home
when eating at my
home.

Rips in My Mood

Hank slams inside the house
rattling my just-cleaned windows.

His friends are still outside
playing
but he's come inside
early.

Usually he plays until dinner
or until Mom calls him in.

He kicks his shoes off
rips his mask off
shoves it deep in his pocket.

How come you're in early?

I want to know.

None of your business!

His voice is the most unmuted it could be.

And every time he looks out the window
it's like his whole face is yelling too.
Even if his mouth is closed.
And quiet.

I made a sign for Café Hummingbird. See?

I tell him to distract him.
I tell him to cheer him up.
I tell him because he might like to help.

(I'd like him to help.)

He's better at drawing than me
and could make a hummingbird
for the sign.

But he doesn't say anything.
He just stares outside.
Outside at his friends.

*Were they mean to you? Maybe you should talk it out
with them.*

I say what I know
teachers used to say to me
when friends are mean at school.

I say what I know
doesn't actually help.
But I don't know
what else to say.
I don't know
how else to help.

I said it's none of your business!

He grabs my sign
and rips it
in
half.

He throws the pieces
back on the table.

I don't even have time
to try
to unmute myself.

Just leave me alone!

he shouts
and bangs back
to our room.
Bangs the door
behind him.
Between us.
Shouts me down.
Shuts me out.

Without saying one word
of all the words
trying to fight their way
out of my mouth

I get up
I get tape
I put the
two halves
of my sign
back together again.

It's "fixed."
But under the tape I can still see the rip
I can still feel the rip
Hank made.

I start over again
and make a brand-new sign.
I don't want my hummingbirds
to see or feel
the rips.

Ready and Waiting

Every day
when I'm not in (not real) school
I sit at the kitchen table
and stick my eyes
on the bright red feeders
sucked to the window.

I don't look at my brother
back outside playing with his friends again.

I only look at the feeder so
when the hummingbirds come
I won't miss them.

Shouting into My Face

I think my mute button must be broken.
I tap it on and off
on and off
on and off
saying

    Mute Mute Mute

because if it's broken
no one will ever be able
to hear me
even when I want them to.

I test it
while everyone else is talking
and not settling down.

But then I hear

    That's not funny, Archie

by someone leaning in so close to their microphone
it was like a shout through my screen
right in my face.

I leave the classroom meeting room
without telling my mom.

When she finds me playing
not working at (not real) school
I tell her we had internet problems
and that my tablet did something wrong.

Not me.
I didn't do anything wrong.
I am muted.

No hummingbirds yet.

Still no hummingbirds.

Dark Writing

Today my letters come out
pressed hard
dark
thick
and
full
of
my
dark
thick
feelings.

Deep Scars

I could take my pencil
in my hand
and wrap
my fingers
around it
like a fist.

And then scrub it
all over the page
hard hard hard

until the pages
underneath
all the other pages
felt it too.

Like a punch
like a bruise

like a scar

(Sorry)

I am sorry, notebook.

I turned some pages over

until the dents were gone
and the scar
was healed.

You're okay now.

(Another Sorry)

I am sorry, pencil.

You're too nice
too special
to be used
for angry writing.

But you made my letters
my angriness
so dark
and real
and easy
to write.

It made me feel better.

I hope the sharpener
made you feel better.

You have a point again.

(That's something my PE teacher said: *Did you hear the
joke about the pencil? It didn't have any point!*)

But you do.

Muted Mom

When she was checking my work
my mom found my angry pages.

She sat there
just looking
saying nothing.
Her mouth was on mute
just like my screen.

I Am the Worst/I Am the Best

I don't like it when my mom
says nothing.
Especially when I keep expecting her to
say something.
To yell
to punish
to take away my TV watching
my LEGO playing
my extra extra extra screen time.

But she doesn't.
She stays mute.
And I can tell
by her nose
(red and swollen)
that she's been crying.

That I made her cry.

When she comes to tuck me in
I hold her tight tight tight
around her neck.

I press my cheek against hers.
I don't let her go.

I don't want her to cry

the tears that made her nose red
the tears that I made
that made her nose red
and I don't know what
to do to make it better
and take away the before
so she isn't crying in the after.

"Sorry" is too small of a word
to take away the before.

So I grab up all my feelings
and I whisper

   I love you so much I want to eat your flesh.

For some reason
that makes my mom laugh
so hard
she cries anyway
but the tears come while laughing.

I made her cry again.
I like this way better.

Books Full of Hummingbirds

My mom can finally go to the library.
After months and months of being closed
for safety
months of no new books
months of waiting
months of worrying
the library has books for us again.
If you make an appointment
and wear a mask
and get your books from an opening
in the door
and stay six feet away
and use sanitizer
before
and after.

They worked hard

Mom said

to reopen for everyone.

She sniffles a bit.

*I'm just a little emotional. To do something that was
once normal . . .*

I hug her
because I know how it feels
to miss the way everything was
before.

Mom sets the stack of library books
on the kitchen table.

It's a big pile
full of hummingbirds.
Hummingbird books
I asked for.

There are no hummingbirds
at the window
yet.

But there are
hundreds of hummingbirds
in these pages
now.

Facts about Hummingbirds:

empress
pufflegs
sunangels
woodstar
mountain-gem
scintillant
barbthroats
copper-rumped

are species of hummingbird
I did not know before.
I know them all now.

Facts about Hummingbirds:

When they're resting
which they don't do very much
a hummingbird's heart
beats 600 beats per minute.

When I am resting
which I don't do very much
my heart
beats 66 beats per minute.

When they're flying around
which they do a lot
a hummingbird's heart
beats 1,260 beats per minute.

When I'm running around the house
which I'm not supposed to do
I can't measure my heartbeat
because I'm too busy

running around the house.

It's Our Room. Our. Room.

My brother and I share a room.
Sometimes
    a lot of times
when we're not sleeping
my brother makes me
go away.

    Leave me alone!

he says.
I tell him

    This is my room too! I get to be here!

The room is loud with anger
until my mom makes me leave.

    Give him some alone time

she says.

    We all need alone time. Especially now.

People *keep* saying that
but it doesn't feel true.
Why would anyone *want* to be alone?
Why would anyone *want* to be lonely?

I don't need *alonely* time
so when it's my turn
in the room
when the room is empty
I don't go in.

Instead I go to the couch
or the kitchen table
or the porch
wherever my brother is.
He's staying inside more
and more now.
More chances for me
to get him
to be
more with me.

I sit close.
I talk close.
I am close
so he knows I am there.
Then he shoves me
away
so I am not there
anymore.

They Taught Us Sharing Is Caring

My brother doesn't like
to share
anything of his.

Not his LEGOs.
Not his friends.
Not his space.

He listens to an audiobook
in our (shared) room.

I walk in.
He snaps his headphones over his ears
not even sharing the sound.

Facts about Hummingbirds:

They keep all other
hummingbirds out
of their territory.

They don't like sharing with trespassers.

HUMMINGBIRD

There's a hummingbird there!
There's a hummingbird here!
There's a hummingbird eating there and here!

It stops for just an eye blink
whipping its wings
in what I can't quite see
but I know
(because I read)
(in my essential library books)
is a figure-8 pattern.

A gray-brown blur of 8s.

```
8              8
 88           88
 8888      8888
  8888  8888
```

No other kind of bird can do this.

Hummingbirds can!

My hummingbird does!

Hummingbird Sounds

click-chirp-click-chirp-click-click-click-click

That is the noise
my hummingbird makes
to tell me she is here.

To tell me she's hungry.
To tell me she's about to sip
our homemade nectar
from Café Hummingbird.

When I hear her
I stop everything
I'm doing.

I try to sneak creep
                    quiet
                        careful
                            slow
                                to the window
                                to get a better look.

But she's so fast.
She zips
up and away
before I can get close.

Still, Close, Quiet

This morning
I stand close
and still
and waiting
at the window.

I want to be there
when my hummingbird
comes here.

It's so hard
to stand
this
still.

It's so hard
to wait
for something
to happen.

I want to
run scream yell my head off jump up and down and be
loud and moving everywhere

but that might scare her away

so I take a deep breath

the way my PE teacher
taught for *mindfulness*.
I put my hand on my chest
feeling my heartbeats
counting my heartbeats
a-gain
and
a-gain
and
a-gain.

I count the beats
count the beats
count the beats
count the beats.

It sounds like it's saying

    I hope I hope I hope.

Slow

and

steady

I watch an ant
try to find a way
into the house

through a hole
in our screen.

I smell a hidden breeze
shake tiny pink flowers
down to the ground.

I hear the bark
shuffle off
our myrtle trees.

click-chirp-click-chirp-click-click

Out of the corner
of my eye
I see a whisper whip
of bright green

and a flash a flick
of red.

My hummingbird is here!
My heartbeat is thwalloping!
Hopebeat!
Hopebeat!
Hopebeat!

More Hummingbird Sounds

hummmm
thrummmm
delicate drummmm

is what the vibrating window says
when my hummingbird
comes near.

Facts about My Hummingbird:

We named her *Ruby*.

Me and my mom thought
that was the best name
for a little hummingbird
with a little bit of red
on her throat
and a little bit of red
on her head.

That little bit of head
that is red
is called
a crown.

A crown
of rubies.

A crown
for Ruby.

Migration Means to Go Far Away
for a Long Time or Forever

I read
all about the
hummingbirds that live
near us
and told my mom
all about them.

We want to learn what
kind of hummingbird
Ruby is.

Is she an Anna's hummingbird
the fastest hummingbird of all?

I don't want her to be a Rufous
because they are aggressive
violent
and much meaner
than other
hummingbirds.

(They're also orange-er
than other hummingbirds.
Is that what orange is?
Is orange mean

violent
and aggressive?)

I want Ruby to be an Anna's
because unlike all the others
Anna's hummingbirds
don't go away.

They don't migrate
to warmer weather
and leave us
alone.

Not Sharing

Maybe she's a Calliope hummingbird with a pink beak

Hank says.

He looks over my shoulder
without my permission.

*I read about Calliope in the Percy Jackson books. She
was . . .*

I cover my book
with both hands.
I want to mute the book
when he's around.

Hummingbirds drink nectar?

Hank asks.

He can read the words
through my fingers.

That's what the Greek gods drink, you know.

I snap my book shut.
Now all my hummingbirds

and everything about them
is on mute to Hank.

I don't want
to share Ruby
with my brother

OR his stupid Greek gods.

Not Caring

My mom buys two more feeders.

*It would be fun to see if we can observe them from our
bedroom windows too*

she says.

I help her with the one
outside my bedroom window.

That way I can glare
at my brother
on the other side of the window.

He's watching us
from inside
and my frown
and growl-mouth
tell him

Stay away from my territory!

My angry eyes
are the exclamation point.

So he knows
I really mean it.

No

Every morning at 10:00
during school
we get 15 minutes
of break.

Our teacher calls it
recess.

At (real) school
it would be called
snack recess.

And we'd all go outside
and we'd be with friends
eating our snacks
and running around.

Playing together.

My mom tells me

    Go out out out out! Get some exercise!

She wants me to
scooter
or bike

or run
the whole time.

No playing.
No snacks.
No friends.

She says I need to get more exercise.
That more exercise will make me
feel better.
Make me happier.
Make me forget about
no playing.
No snacks.
No friends.
No (real) school.

Trees Are Exercise

When you spend enough time
climbing
in trees
you learn that
bees do have knees
woodpeckers hate checkers
and bark
actually
does
what it says
it does.

More Tree Thoughts

With one foot on a branch the other on the trunk
I stop climbing our magnolia tree
long enough
to realize
something:
a *deciduous* tree
is a tree
that decided
it was old enough

to

take

off

its

own

leaves.

Today
in the
hot sun
I am a

decidedly
deciduous tree.

And

one

by

one

by

one

I drop
all my leaves
to the ground.

When my purple spotted underwear
floats down
my mom shouts

ARCHIE!

And I hide in the green
of the (real) leaves
and giggle.

Facts about Hummingbirds:

Sometimes

Blue jays

Eat

Them

White Skies, Angry Eyes

Outside the sky is strange
and white.

Not blue
with white clouds.

Not gray
with overcast fog.
But hot
and waiting
and breathless.

And so white
and so dense
with that thick cover of
white strangeness
I can't even see
where the sun is.

But I can see
where the blue jays are.

I let them know I have my angry eyes
and serious eyebrows*
on them.

(*Eyebrows tell a lot of jokes but they can be serious when they need to be.
Especially when it comes to blue jays eating hummingbirds.)

Zoom Waiting Rooms

I was so busy
watching the blue jays
with my angry eyes
that I come back late
from break.

Not too late.
Just a little.

But when I try to go to my
online classroom
I can't get in.

The screen just
spins and spins and spins
and I
sit
sit
sit

alone.

In virtual school
there is no door
for you to knock on
to say

I'm here—please let me in!

When I am
finally let in
my teacher is
almost done reading
our book of the week.

I missed all the reading.
I missed the ending.
I missed out.

I Missed and Wasn't Missed

I raise my hand
and wait
until my teacher asks
if I have a question.

I say

    I missed the ending of the book.

She says

    Oh I can't hear you. Can you unmute yourself?

I unmute myself and say
louder and angrier

    I missed the ending of the book.

I want her to understand
I don't want to have to say more
I don't want to explain.

    I missed the ending of the book and I'm sad and I feel
    left out and alone.

I want her to know that
without me saying it.

But she says

> *I'm sorry about that. I didn't realize you were stuck in the waiting room after break.*

No one
in the class
not even my teacher
realized I was missing.

I mute myself again.

Muted and Invisible

For the rest of the day
I put my head
down
on my desk.

My mom tells me
my teacher can't
see me
on my screen
when I do that.

I tell her
my teacher doesn't
see me
on my screen
whatever I do.

I Used to Like Books

Hank places a
book on my
(not real school) desk.

It's old
and kind of beat up.
It looks
wrinkled
torn
and very tired.

He says

> *I heard what happened in your school today. This is*
> *the same book your teacher was reading. It's been on*
> *my bookshelf forever.*

I want to tell him to mind his own business.
I want to rip his old wrinkled used book in half
just like he did to my old Café Hummingbird sign.

Hank says

> *If you want, you can read the parts you missed on your*
> *own*

then walks away.
He doesn't even wait for me
to answer.

He leaves me
on my own.
To read his book
on my own.

On my own
on my own

on my lone

alone.

I shove the book
far under
my bed.

Now *it's*
on its own.

When the Storms Come

We don't get many thunderstorms.
We do get lots of rain
in winter
but it doesn't come with the kind of storm that
crashes and flashes.

When thunder rolls around
the whole family usually has to ask

> *What was that?*
> *An airplane?*
> *An earthquake?*

We don't know thunderstorms
enough
to know them
well.

Tonight
when it is pale gray
with not-quite morning
a big storm comes.

Splits of lightning
flash under my sleeping eyes
and slams of thunder

scrabble me out of my covers
to my parents' bed.

Hank would normally call me a baby
for being scared
for running to Mom and Dad
but he's right behind me.

As if he doesn't want to be
left behind
or left alone.

Scared Inside

I'm old enough
not to be
but I am scared
of the thunderstorms.
I'm not used to them.

My brother is next to me.

    It's just noise and light

he says.

    We're safe inside.

Safe inside.
Safe inside.
Safe inside.

Alone Like a Hummingbird

The storm crouches
over our house for hours.

The winds blow a lot.
But it rains only a little.
Barely enough for Ruby
to take the kind of shower
hummingbirds need
to keep their feathers
neat and clean.

She will have to find a puddle
or a leaf filled up
like a tub
to take a better bath.

I stick my nose close
to the window screen
to smell the rain.

It smells like
wet
and mud
and loud
gray skies.

I wonder

where does my hummingbird
go during loud storms?

Hummingbirds spend most of their life
alone.

Very alone.

I hope my hummingbird
finds a tree
or a branch
at least a sheltered twig
where she feels safe
and inside
and not scared of the noise.
Not scared of the flashing
crashing light.

Burning Hot

The next morning is
hot hot hot hot.

Other places
have sweaters
in October.

California
has heat waves
in October.

When I stick my nose close
to the screen again
I don't smell rain.

I smell smoke.
Burning wood
like a campfire.
But it smells way too big
for a campfire.
It's way too much.
It's out of control.

It is not marshmallows
or hot dogs
that are burning.
It is trees

it is land
it is homes.

The storm
with its crashing wind
and flashing lightning
and not enough not enough not enough
splashing rain
left wildfires behind.

The storm can't hurt me inside.
But it can hurt
too many things
outside.

Wildfire Season Shouldn't Be Allowed to Be a Season

We didn't used to have
so many fires.

We had "fire season"
and we knew that was a time
every year
when we had to be careful.

When there were days
dry days
windy days
hot and brown-feeling days
when we shouldn't light campfires
and shouldn't shoot fireworks.
When we shouldn't do anything
that might cause a spark
and burn down an entire forest.
And all the animals in it.

But those days
used to be
just a few days.
Just a few weeks.
Now they are
too many
months.

And the fires come every year
and stay
and stay
and stay
and burn
burn
burn
burn
burn.

And at school
we send cards to firefighters.
To thank them for saving us.
To thank them for protecting us.
To thank them
to thank them
to thank them.

We didn't used to have
so many fires.

Now we have too many.

I Don't Like Change of Any Kind

My parents say that
more fires
and less rain
every year
is making
the climate change.

That what we are doing (too much)
as humans
is making the climate change.

Too many cars.
Too many factories.

Not enough trees.
Not enough bees.

Which means even
more fires
and even
less rain.

I get dizzy thinking
that fires are burning and destroying
because of climate change
and that the climate is changing
because fires are burning and destroying

life that can stop
climate change.

The forests are crying out
the icebergs are having meltdowns
the earth is screaming
for help
for attention.

But no one is listening.
Because everyone has
the planet
on mute.

Water to Survive

Last night I couldn't sleep.
I kept thinking about all the animals
in the forest and how scared
they must be.
All alone
in the fires.

Ruby
alone
scared
so tiny.

My mom stroked my arm
for a long time
until I could feel
calm sink into
my skin.

She said

> During wildfires, the animals know to run away from
> danger. We can help them by making it easier to find
> water if they come this way. It will help them survive.

Today I fill big
metal bowls full of
cold

fresh
water.

Big metal bowls
full of hope.
Full of life.

My mom takes them outside
and asks me
where I think
they should go.

I tell her by the curb
in case the animals are too scared
to come close
    and under the magnolia tree
    with its big creamy blossoms
        and next to the side gate
        where they can sleep in the shade.

I think of being scared.
I think of sleeping in shade
    of needing to feel safe.

Needing hope.

I take a deep breath
I put my hand on my heart
I count the hopebeats

count the hopebeats
count the hopebeats
count the hopebeats.

And I think of how
there are
so many
different ways
we can
survive.

When Breathing Is Too Hard

My mom goes outside
with a mask.
My brother goes outside
with a mask.

They wear masks
not for the COVID
but for the smoke
and the ash
in the air.

I stay inside
with my inhaler
because my mom says
even with a mask
my asthma makes the air
more dangerous
for me.

And the smoke still
attacks my lungs.

Together
they refill
Ruby's feeders.

My brother

fills
my
hummingbird's
feeders.

He comes inside.
He brushes ash
out of his hair.

He looks at me.

I don't look at him back.

> *I was just helping*

he says.

> *I don't WANT your help! You're always telling me to mind my own business so why don't you mind YOUR own business? My hummingbirds are MINE! MY business!*

I yell all of it.
I get all of it
out.

> *They're not just your—*

But he stops. He leaves.

I got all of it out

and now I feel
empty.

Facts about Boogers:

Boogers should not be allowed
to be gray.

But that's what mine are
after seven days
of smoky air.

Facts about Hummingbirds:

They are the smallest birds
of all.
They lay the smallest eggs
of all.

They have the smallest lungs
of all.

More Facts about Hummingbirds:

They don't have inhalers.

Facts about My Hummingbird:

I haven't seen Ruby in a very long time.

Holding Myself Together with Tears

I stand close to the window
and think
hummingbird thoughts
to myself.

I think about how hummingbirds
are the only birds
that can hover.
They are the helicopters
of birds.

I think about the huge
helicopters that are
dropping water
on the wildfires.

I think about how hummingbirds
have a body temperature
of 104°.

If my temperature was
that high
I'd have a fever.

And they'd make me
get a test
not at school

for spelling or for math
but at the doctor's office.

A COVID test.
A test where a negative
is good
but a positive
is bad.

Bad enough
that I might get
sick enough
and not be able to
breathe enough
on my own.

I think about Ruby
on her own.

My cheeks feel fever-y now
as tears hit them.

I think about how hummingbirds
use spiderwebs
to hold their tiny nests
together.

Spiderwebs are the
strongest stuff

in nature.
Stronger even
than steel.

I think about how I wish
I had spiderwebs
to hold my heart
together.

Wishes and Brothers and Dandelions and Nests

Even though the smoke is gone for today
even though his friends are still outside
my brother
comes inside.

He's holding a dandelion.

> *I read that hummingbirds use dandelion fluff in their*
> *nests to keep them warm*

he says

He sees my angry eyes
and spins his wordstogetherfast
before I can get my mad words
untangled.

> *I'm sorry I read your book without asking. I know it's*
> *yours. I was just interested*
> *because you are*

he says.

Hank has never been interested in what I'm interested in
because he was always interested first.

By the time I discover it

he's done with it.
Over it.
Bored.

But not this time.

My words lose
the mad
my words loosen
untangled.

　　It's okay

is all I say.

　　I read something else about your hummingbirds

he says.

I hear the *your*
and it makes me listen more
and angry
less.

　　I read that at high altitudes they can capture extra
　　oxygen with every breath. Maybe Ruby is doing that in
　　the smoke.

Then Hank

holds out the dandelion
fluffy
and round.
Soft with hope.

I thought you might want this wish. For Ruby.

Then he turns and walks to the porch.
He opens the screen door and holds it
for me
for me to blow my wish
outside.

I stand on the steps next to him
I take as deep of a breath
as my inhaler gives me
and blow my wish
to Ruby.

Me and my brother
stand on the steps
together
watching the dandelion seeds
together.
Breathing

together.

Masks to Protect Each Other

Sitting at the table
that was once
my play table
and is now my
(not real) school desk
Hank helps me.

He shows me tricks
and secrets
and virtual backgrounds
for my classes.

He shows me
a way to draw
on my tablet.

He shows me how
we can draw
together
on our tablets.

We laugh.
We are silly.

This is another day
when I realize
his friends

are outside
together
but my brother
is inside
with me.

Why aren't you playing with them?

I ask.

He frowns
but not at me.

They kept not wearing their masks. They said they were too annoying. I told them you have asthma and that getting COVID could be even more dangerous for you, but also that any of us could get really, really sick. And that any of us can give COVID to other people. But they kept not wearing them. So now I'm not playing with them.

My brother's heart
is made of spiderwebs.

Story Time

In our room
my brother lies
on his bed
and stares
at the ceiling.

In our room
I sit
on my bed
and stare
at my brother.

We can hear his friends
outside playing
together.

> *Without you! Without you! Without you!*

is not at all what
they're yelling.

But it feels like
it's exactly what
they're yelling.

My brother stares

at the hummingbird feeder
on our window.

> *I always thought the red feathers on her throat looked
> like sequins*

he whispers.

> *I miss her.*

I reach for the book
shoved far under
my bed.

I pretend to be
my teacher
and I read it to
my whole class
of one brother.

Orange

The smoke came back
because the fires never left.

The fires have been burning for days now.
Burning all our days now.

The sky is supposed to be orange only
at sunset
or at sunrise.

The sky should not be orange
at breakfast
or lunch
or (not real) recess.

The sky should not be orange
and feel
like night
all day
even though
bedtime is
hours away.

The sky should not be orange
and smell like smoke

and sound silent
and feel still.
Like everything
is scared.
Like everyone
is holding their breath.
Like no one
can breathe.

The sky should not be orange
and make my dad tape
the cracks
around our windows
and doors
to keep the smoke out
and our air in.

The sky should not be orange
and make our eyes sting
and our throats burn.

The sky makes me throw
my orange crayon
in the trash.

I know what orange is now.

It's what the sky should
not be.

Not today.
Not ever.

Orange Again

My brother sits on my bed.
I roll away from him.
So he doesn't see the tears
that roll down my cheeks.
So he doesn't see another reason
to think I'm a baby.

Orange isn't a bad color

he says.

Orange is the color of tangerines and carrots.

I don't move.

It's the color of Dad's university

he says

and Mom's pumpkin bread.

I roll toward him.

The one with the chocolate chips?

I ask.

Yes

he says.

> *Orange is the color of sweet potato fries with extra*
> *spice at Gott's Roadside Diner.*
> *Orange is the color of Halloween and leaves falling*
> *and the cuddly big cat next door.*
> *And look what I found in one of your hummingbird*
> *books.*

He flips the slick pages
looking
searching
finally finding.

> *Look, hummingbirds like orange flowers!*

He points.
I read the caption out loud.

> *An Anna's hummingbird visits the hard-to-find fire*
> *poppy. The fire poppy is part of a group of wildflowers*
> *known as "fire followers." Fire followers specifically*
> *grow in the burn scars wildfires leave behind in the*
> *earth.*

I think of flowers

growing
in scars.

Making something
beautiful
out of something
ugly.

My brother uncurls his hand.
My orange crayon.

> *I thought you might want this again sometime. To
> color in the oranges you like.*

Only the Delicious Things

I'm setting the table:
—first forks
then folded napkins like beds
for the knives and spoons to lie down on—
when it happens.

My dad comes through the front door
with big brown bags clutched in both hands.

He shakes the bags
which crinkle
and steam
with familiar smells.

   It's Friday—it's Café Borrone night!

My brother runs
down the hall.
His mouth is wide
with wonder
and hunger.

   They're open again?

   Just for takeout for now

Dad explains.

Takeout is enough for now.
Takeout is essential for now.

My mom is smiling
grinning
giggling
as she helps unpack
the bags
and boxes.

I only ordered the most delicious things.

Hot grilled squid
with lemon.

Gouda and ham sandwiches
on fat
greasy focaccia.
A messy fish sandwich
dripping with slaw
salty with bacon

all made by cooks
back in the kitchen
feeding us
filling our stomachs

and our hearts
with mouthfuls of hope.

Everything tastes *more* itself
than it ever did before.

The squid is squiddier
the bacon crunchier
and the grease from the fat focaccia
makes my chin shine.

We bring books
and
puzzles
and
things to draw
and
stories to tell
one another.

We are silly.
We laugh.
We are all together
in the same room.

My food is so happy
it sings to me
in my mouth.

My brother hums with me
and then says

    I think Archie is a hummingbird when he eats.

My mom hums too
she says

    We're a whole house of hummingbirds.

Then we all look to the window
together
at the empty feeder
full of nectar
but not full of Ruby.

    Just wait until the smoke clears. She'll be back

my dad says.

We are all quiet.

    Do you know how smart hummingbirds are?

my dad asks.

We all wait.

    I read in one of Archie's books that hummingbirds

are tiny, but their brains make up 4.2% of their body weight. Compared to other birds, that's the largest proportion of brain size to body weight. And humans? Our human brains make up only 2% of our body weight.

We keep waiting.

Dad sighs.

He loves to tell us number-y things.
We love to hear them (mostly).
But we don't always understand them.

Dad tries one last time.

Ruby is smart. She knows you're her friend and will come back for food. Don't lose hope.

I take a deep breath
I put my hand on my heart
I count the hopebeats.
Don't lose hope.
Don't lose hope.
Don't lose hope.

Facts about Hummingbirds:

They remember every flower they've ever visited.

Facts about Me:

Once I dressed up as a pink flower for Halloween.

Facts I Don't Know:

Ruby will remember me.

Please Come Home

The sky stopped being orange
all day every day and
the air is no longer coated with haze
and when I breathe in
my tongue doesn't
taste smoke anymore.

Every day
when I'm not in
(not real) school
I stand next to the window.

If Ruby sees my face
at the window
she will know
she is home.

The ducks at the pond
in the park
might not recognize me
in my mask
as my half-self
but inside the house
there are no masks.

Ruby will see me.
Ruby will come.

But Ruby
still stays away.

Jolted

It is not a storm
that wakes me up
with a jump
and a gasp
and a sit-straight-up-in-bed.

At first
I don't know
what it is
why I am awake
in the dark.
With my head
fuzzy with sleep.

I look across the shadows
past my brother
(snoring)
to the window.

And I remember.

I remember that we forgot
to fill the feeders.

Clock Beyond Time

It is late
so late
I feel like there are numbers
on the clock
I've never seen before.

But Ruby's feeders
are empty.
And they can't
stay empty
even if it's so late
the clock is
inventing new numbers
no one's ever heard of.

If Ruby came back to empty feeders
she might leave.

She might think
we left.

She might think
we (I)
don't
love
her.

NOISY

In the kitchen
I sneak around
trying not to make
a sound.

But everything everything
is
so
so
SO
loud.

For once
I want to be
silent.

My socked feet
scraffle!
across the wood floor.

The glass jar of nectar
clinks!
when I set it down on
the black granite counter.

The clear nectar
glorps!

when I pour it
carefully
carefully
into a small spouted
measuring cup.

The refrigerator door
slucks!
open
and
snicks!
closed.

Even the light
inside the refrigerator
seems to scream
that I'm out of bed
and doing something
I shouldn't be.

I Am Not Scared

I ease the front door
open and leave it ajar
the tiniest bit behind me.
Not enough for anyone to notice
if they also jolt awake
and investigate.
Just crack enough
to slip me back in.

Outside in the darker than dark
I should be scared
of the shadows hiding something
of the silence speaking loud
in that creepy
quiet
shout.

But tonight
I am not scared.

Tonight
Ruby needs me.

And the shadows
the night
the dark
surround me

hide me
help me.

I'm my quietest
slipping by my parents'
window
which is
wide to the night.

I peek in
making my head a
sudden shadow
in the moonlight flooding
their sheets.
I duck.

I fill my bedroom feeder last.
The patio outside my window is darker
than everywhere else.

The Smell of Cold

Tonight I can smell
that the weather is getting colder.
Colder and smellier.

Not *bad* smellier.
Not smoke smellier.
But smelly like crunchy brown leaves
and hard-cased acorns
split-cracked by saving squirrels.
Chilly breezes
soft hoodies
and cider
for breakfast.

We don't ever get snow here
but sometimes when I wake up
and my window has been open
all night
the cold in my room
smells white
and bright blue.

The way I dream
snow would smell.

It's fall and the leaves

are falling
and in the fall
every day
smells new.

Dead

A dead leaf
is curled
around the feeder perch
that Ruby only sometimes uses.
Ruby likes to hover-feed more.
She doesn't really rest.

I reach out a finger
to brush
the dead leaf
away.

To make sure
this dead leaf
doesn't steal
Ruby's perch.

But my reaching finger
doesn't touch
a dried
dead leaf.

It touches
a soft
still
something.

I snatch my hand back I don't know what I touched

. . .

My brain said

    Leaf.

But my fingers said

    Not leaf!

And my brain and my fingers are arguing
while my eyes squint and strain
and try to break up the fight
with more information.

A light flashes
then a voice slashes
the dark open.

    What is that?

Is She Dead?

My brother stands at the gate
to the patio
one hand over his mouth
the other holding a flashlight.

The flashlight beam
on the red feeder
shows us the
soft
still
something
is a hummingbird
hanging
upside down
from the perch
on the red feeder.

Is she dead?

My brother is
at my side
gripping my arm.

I open my mouth
but my voice isn't
in there.

I stare at Ruby
soft
still
something

something

something.

There's something
in my head
I just need to find it.
I need to find it now.
I search through all of my brain.

Need to Think. Count the Beats.

There's something

I say—

Tor—

and stop.
I can't remember
how it ends.
How any of this will end.

My brother
digs his fingers
into my arm.

Tornado?

he says.

We don't have tornadoes here!

I shake my head.
It's not tornadoes.
It's like tornadoes but
also not like tornadoes.

Torpedo?

my brother says.

    Do you think she looks like a torpedo hanging there?

I shake off his hand
I have to think
he's not letting me think
shoving words in my
head that shouldn't be there.

I take a deep breath
I put my hand on my heart
I count the beats
count the hopebeats
count the hopebeats
count the hopebeats.

I find the word in my head.

    Torpor!

I say.

    Ruby's not dead—she's in torpor!

Facts about Hummingbirds:

In order to conserve energy
at night
hummingbirds can go into a
deep sleep called torpor.

They lower their temperature
they lower their heart rate
sometimes they hang
upside down
and look
dead

but they aren't.

Don't Touch

My brother doesn't believe me.

Are you sure? She looks dead.

My brother reaches out
with a questioning finger.
I know it would be
a gentle finger
but I stop him anyway.

*We shouldn't touch her. She's in a deep sleep. We need
to leave her alone.*

I really want to pet her
myself
to touch her feathers
to feel her crown
her beak
her heart.

I wish we could pet her
but I know we should not
even if we are gentle.

I Wish Other Books Had Warned Me First

This is the part
of many books
where an animal
dies.

This is the part
of many books
where the kid living inside the book

and the kid reading
and living
outside the book

(and sometimes even the grown-ups
inside and outside the book)

learn a lesson about life
and how it ends
as life has to end

in death.

This is the part of many books
where tears fall
and hugs wrap you up.

This is the part of many books

where the book
wants to make you
feel something.

But I never have to
read about death
to know about death.

Or to know
how I feel
about death.

Death is everywhere
and all around us
during the pandemic.

You don't even have
to read about it
to know about it.

And in that hummingbird heartbeat
moment
death did not have to happen
for me to
feel everything.

When Dreams Feel Real

I wake up in the morning
and remember
snatches
flashes
of last night.

I trip out of bed
climb over my
brother's grumbling
blanket mountains
and fling the shades
wide.

The feeder is empty.
Was Ruby ever
there?

I press my face
against the screen
which smells like thin metal
and dirt.
I search the ground
under the feeder
and see nothing.

Did last night happen?

my brother asks.

His eyes are sleepy
but awake.

Was Ruby really on the feeder like she was dead?

I wonder
how we could have both had
the same dream.

Trying to Stay Awake

I am so tired from last night's
(not) dream that I can
barely
pay attention
to my daily math
my reading log
my daily language
or anything else.

My mom says that
distance learning school days
are more exhausting than
real school days.

Too much going
nowhere
instead of going
somewhere
or everywhere.

It seems like it would be more
exhausting to go everywhere.

But I'd like to go
anywhere but here.

Especially if it's in my bed.

Still Fall

Ms. Peak Is Missing

I staaaaaare out the window
waiting for Ruby
looking for Ruby
hoping for Ruby.

I stare so long
my eyes get fuzzy
blurry
heavy.

    Ms. Peak, you're frozen!

someone
maybe Alejandro
says.

They shout it.
My eyes are jolted from the
window screen
to my
tablet screen.

Ms. Peak's center square flicks off.

    MS. PEAK DISAPPEARED!

someone

maybe Steven
yells.

More someones say the same thing over and over and
over
like everyone wants a chance to say it
like every time someone new says it

    MS. PEAK DISAPPEARED!
    MS. PEAK DISAPPEARED!
    MS. PEAK DISAPPEARED!
    MS. PEAK DISAPPEARED!

it makes everyone gasp even louder.

We wait.
This has happened before.
Ms. Peak always comes back.

But not this time.

We are all unmuted.

And things
get
loud.

                  Eli leans into his tablet
                        and sings.

(I don't know what he's singing
because Chloe is up
and dancing
and her footprints
are stomping through her microphone.)
                    Will R. tells everyone it's dinnertime
                and he's having pizza.
(It's not dinnertime.
It's only 9:12 in the morning.
I checked.)
            There's a baby crying
                in someone's house
        beyond their tablet.
                                Steven shouts

I have a diamond!

I have a diamond!
                    I have a diamond!

        Mute yourself if you want to see a
    diamond!

I mute.
I wait.
No diamond.
I unmute.
                    Eli's mom
                (who is a teacher

but not our teacher)
            is trying to get everyone to mute themselves
and do their work

                                    but no one is
listening
      and she can't make us
                        listen or mute
                  because she's not the host
of our meeting and
        Eli is leaping
                        leaping
                                    LEAPING
      behind her
      and she can't quite grab   his superhero shirt
                                          while she leans
into
                  his tablet and

tries to make things calm.

      Zoey changed her name

(we're not allowed to change our names).

            And now instead of Zoey
      her square says BLAHBLABLAH
Vividh and Linus are in the chat box

but they don't know what to write
                                so they fill it with emojis
instead.

And I have an idea.
I take my tablet
to the window.
To show them Ruby's feeders.
I hold my screen to the screen.
But no one is listening
or watching
anyone else
but themselves.
But I don't care.
This is the most fun
I've had all year.

Then through all the noise and the face-making and the
emoji typing
I
hear
something
else.

Ruby, Again

click-chirp-click-chirp-click-click-CHIRP

She stops for just an eye blink
sipping her nectar
whipping her wings
in what I can't quite see
but know
(because I know I know I know)
is a figure-8 pattern.

A gray-brown blur of 8s.

```
8                 8
 88               88
  8888       8888
   8888   8888
```

And a whisper whip
of bright green.

She's back

our Ruby has come back
to us!

And I Unmute Myself

Suddenly, I realize
there's silence
the whole class is on mute.
Our teacher is back.

Archie

Ms. Peak says.

*Is that the hummingbird you've been writing about in
class? It looks like a male hummingbird with that red
throat and that proud red crown!
Archie—*

she says because I am still muted

*—what is his name? What is your flying friend's
name?*

I take a deep breath
and I feel my hopebeats

and I unmute myself.

Ruby

I say.

Then I hold my screen up
for the whole class.

I make sure
they can see Ruby
and they can see me.

And they say

    Ooooh!

And

    Look at that bird!

And

    I want a hummingbird feeder!

And

    How did you do that, Archie?

And Ms. Peak lets me
(and only me)
answer all their questions
and tell them all I know.

And they listen.
And they see me.

Sharing Unmuted

It's a morning for me!
It's the day I'm sharing
everything I know
everything I love
everything I've written
about Ruby.

Ms. Peak is dedicating
our entire community circle
to me. And Ruby.

I have pictures
I drew
facts
I collected
a log
I wrote
and a recipe
I made.

I have so much to say
so much to explain
so much to tell.

About the first time I saw Ruby
about how heartbeats became hopebeats

about how that hope was so hard to hold on to when
Ruby was gone.

I can't wait
to get
it all out
like a sigh of
snuggling into bed
on a cold night
when you're the
right amount of sleepy

a sigh of
eating just enough
after being so hungry
for so long

a sigh

of happiness.

One Face

I'm talking
and explaining
and describing
and teaching
and showing
(and smiling)

when Ms. Peak tells me

You can take questions now, Archie.

I'm swiping screens
and seeing faces
and excited eyes
and noticing hands
raised.

And answering questions
that are comments
and questions
that are questions.

More swipes
more hands
more excited eyes
more faces

swipe!

One face

no hands

red eyes
eyes looking down
eyes that are filled
wet
shiny
with lonely
muted
sadness.

Yelling on Top of Your Sadness

I stop everything
about Ruby.

Ms. Peak

I say

I think Zoey has something she needs to say.

Zoey looks up
she looks at me
I look back
I want her to know
I see her sadness.

Oh, Zoey

Ms. Peak says

are you okay?

Zoey shakes her head.

Do you want to tell us something?

Ms. Peak asks.

Can you mute everyone, Ms. Peak? So Zoey can talk?

I ask
because I know
how hard it can be
to talk
when you're sad
and everyone is yelling
over through on top
of your sadness.

This Is Hard for Everyone

Zoey takes in
the kind of breath you need
to stop your mouth from shaking
to stop your tears from welling
to stop your voice from trembling
to be brave enough to
unmute your sadness.

> *I didn't want to interrupt Archie. It's just that when he
> was talking about Ruby being in the fire by herself, it
> made me think . . .*

Zoey stops.
She swallows.
She starts again.

> *It made me think of my mom. My mom got really
> sick. Really really sick. She is in the hospital. All by
> herself. Because we're not allowed to be there with her.
> Everyone keeps telling me that she's going to be okay
> but I still miss her. And I'm scared. Everyone is scared
> and that's even scarier. And I can't see her or hug her
> and I hate all of this so much. I hate being scared and
> sad all the time.*

Ms. Peak wipes her eyes.

I'm so sorry, Zoey. I know how hard this is. Is there anyone else who wants to share?

Hands are raised
voices are unmuted
and everyone is heard.

My dad lost his job.

I can't see my grandparents.

My friends play without me.

We couldn't go on vacation.

I didn't have a birthday party.

My sister stays in her room all day because she can't go to college this year.

My parents fight a lot.

The forest fires made everything worse.

My cat died and I couldn't be with her at the vet when it happened.

I feel lonely all the time.

I miss being at real school.

I don't want any of us
to ever feel muted
again.

Still Here. Together.

Today I shared
a page from my notebook
with the class:

The letter "e" is sometimes silent.
But sometimes the silent "e"
seems to scream when you write it
like eeeeeeeee.
But just in looks
not in sound.
Because it's silent.
But even something
as quiet as silence
can change things.

Just a single silent "e"
changes scar
to scare.

I am scared.
I have scars.

You turn the pages over
and you cannot see
my scars.

But they are still
here.

But I am also
still here.
Ruby is
still here.

And so are you.

We are still here
together.

　　Thank you, Archie

Ms. Peak says.

　　We are still here together.

Ruby Everywhere

I turn on my screen
without help
and touch the link.

A window opens
with Zoey's face in
one square
and my face in
another square.

She smiles.
I smile.

Did you get it yet?

I ask.

Zoey nods
she is still smiling.

*My dad put it up so my mom can see it when she comes
home tomorrow. Are you sure it's okay?*

I nod
I am really
very sure
it's okay.

We had four feeders and really it's okay to just have three. It's all we need.

Zoey leans into the screen.
Her face gets bigger
and happier.

We made the nectar and guess what? We already had a hummingbird visit. And I really think it's Ruby.

I lean into my screen.

I really think it's Ruby too.

Talking and Talking So Much Talking

My parents talked to my doctor
then they talked to my school
about outdoor classrooms
and new ventilation systems
and filters
and hand-washing
and masks.

Then they talked to my doctor
again.

Finally they talked to me
about how I might be happier
and still stay safe
back at school.
Real school.

How my health
isn't just in my lungs
and in my breathing.
My health is also
in my emotions
and how I'm feeling.
My health is
in my heart
and in its hopebeating.

They told me that everything is a balance
and it's hard to always know
the right thing to do.

But they didn't tell me
what I *had* to do.
They asked me
what I *wanted* to do.

And they listened.

(Sort of) Back to School

I'm going back to real school again!
But it won't be like normal school.

I will be in my classroom one week
and distance learn at home the next.

Then back in the classroom the next week.

My dad said it's called "hybrid."

I wrote "hybrid" out with my special pencils.

Then I rearranged the letters so it said "hybird."

I showed it to my dad.

   HI BIRD!

He laughed and said

   Like Ruby!

I told him

   Ruby is everywhere!

He hugged me
tight.

Yes, she is.

New Normal

At school we will wear masks
everywhere.

Have our temperatures taken
(not everywhere thankfully)
but* on our forehead.

Wash
and wash
and wash
and wash
our hands
(and then wash them some more).

I think there will be other
rules too.

New rules
for a not normal school day.

But a new normal school day
with Ms. Peak in person.
And friends
all around.

*Get it? But/butt. I like sneaky jokes.

Different Decisions

Hank isn't going back to in-person school.

When I ask him why
why don't you want to
be in classrooms
see your friends
see your teachers
feel normal again?

He tells me

> *Because this isn't normal. I don't want to be at school*
> *one week and home the next. I don't want to worry*
> *about what will happen if someone in the class gets*
> *COVID and then everyone has to stay home to see if*
> *they have COVID too until it's semi-safe again. Until*
> *someone else gets sick and we have to do it all over*
> *again. I don't like things changing like that. It makes*
> *me feel on edge. At least when I'm at home, I know*
> *what to expect.*

I know that I get worried
and that's where a lot of the angry and sad comes from
but I never knew that Hank did too.

When I tell him this
Hank says

Talking about everything makes it feel more real. So I just don't.

I think about this.
I always talk about my feelings.
As soon as I have them
I have to get them out
loud.
I can't stop them from coming out
even though there are times when I should.

I have gotten used to
the idea that nothing
about me and Hank
is the same
anymore.

I hadn't felt the same
in a long
long
long
time
because everyone was putting me
on mute.

Hank hadn't felt the same
in a long
long
long
time

because he was putting himself
on mute.

I say

    Being on mute—putting feelings on mute—doesn't
work.

Hank sighs.

    You're probably right. Since when did you become the
    big brother?

I smile
inside
and out.

I smile
because
Hank hears me.

First Day Again

My mom packs
my lunch
snack
water bottle
(just like before)
and an extra mask
(just like now).

My dad drives
and I'm excited
under my mask
and over my mask.

I'm excited to wash
and wash
and wash
and wash
my hands.

I'm excited
for all the new rules
because they will mean that
I am there.

I clutch a paper bag in my lap.
In it are hummingbird feeders
for our classroom.

It's been a secret between me
and Ms. Peak.
Until today.

I can't wait.

We pull up at school.

The excitement in my stomach
turns to ALLATONCE scared.

Everything feels strange!
Looks strange!
It's the same school as always
but it's also not the same school at all.
All the teachers are masked
and giving out hand sanitizer
all the kids are masked
and rubbing their hands.
Spots on the sidewalk
show us how to stay
six feet apart.

My heart pounds to remind me what to do.
I take a deep breath.
I clutch the paper bag with one hand
and put the other on my chest.
I feel my hopebeats.

Here

I roll down my window for the school nurse
and move my hair away
from my forehead.
I show her my eyebrows.

She takes my temperature
and her eyes smile
above her orange mask.

Orange like the poppies
blooming
growing
hoping
after the fire.

We're so glad you're here!

she tells me
just like she tells all the kids
and all their foreheads
through all their rolled-down
windows.

I'm here!

A Star Scar

Tonight my parents took us out into the

dark
green
mountains.

Away from all the lights in our town
that make the stars so hard
to see.

We need darkness
to see the light.

There are other cars
and other families (with masks)
out there too.

We keep our distance
but wave at them.
We don't know them.
But we wave.

We wave a lot more now
at people we don't know.
Because the masks can't show our smiles.
So we wave instead.

We do more
instead of less.

We've been out here before (without masks)
to see meteor showers
or planets moving closer together
before they move apart again.

But this time
we all hold hands
when we look up
and this time
when we look up
we see the Milky Way

and it is so very thick with stars.

I've seen the Milky Way in pictures
but this is the first time
I can see it right there
with my own eyes.

It looks like a scar
to me.
Like something
big
and horrible
and unfair
came as a nightmare

and slashed the sky open
leaving a gash
behind.

An emptiness.
A wide far-apartness.
A loneliness.

But then
the stars all gathered
together
and knitted the pieces of the sky back
together
and with their light
they healed it
together
making it stronger
and brighter
than it ever was
before.

Together.

I put my hand on my heart
I think of *Ruby* in my heart

I think of

my family

my teacher
my friends
my (new normal) school
the color orange
trees to climb
telling jokes
new ways to have birthdays
special pencils
the stars
eyebrows
and hummingbirds

together
in my heart

I count my
hopebeats.

AUTHOR'S NOTE

When the pandemic started in late winter of 2020 and we all had to stay inside and wear masks and keep our distance from friends and family, I started putting poems up in our front window. The following poem is one of them. I wanted to reach out to people the only way I knew how: with my words. I wanted to do something to help. I hope this last poem and this book help us remember what we went through, and I hope it helps you with whatever you might be going through now.

You are here.
It's okay
to feel
weird.

It's okay
to hate
what's happening.

It's okay
to grieve
what we've lost.

It's okay
It's okay
It's okay

Now is the time to
find
yourself in
the stars.

Now is the time to
shout
your secrets to
the silence.

Now is the time to
remember
who you are
who we are

who we will
be again.

ACKNOWLEDGMENTS

This book has been such a wonderful and fulfilling journey from drafting to submission to revisions to publication. First I want to thank my agent, Jordan Hamessley, for never giving up and for ultimately leading our team of two to success on this. Your support and steadfast belief in me and Archie will stay with me forever. Second, my amazing editor, Alex Borbolla: you are the editor I've been searching for since I started writing children's literature. I have your edit letter for this book taped above my desk so I can always draw strength from your encouraging words. I know we will do more things together and I cannot wait for that. I also want to thank the entire team at Bloomsbury Children's: assistant editor Kei Nakatsuka, senior production editor Diane Aronson, assistant art director Jeanette Levy, cover artist Karyn S. Lee, and *Hummingbird Season*'s thoughtful copyeditor (you know who you are)—all of you have contributed so much to make this book more beautiful, inside and out, than I could have dreamed it would be. I am truly blown away by the attention to detail and the sheer brilliance of craft you all put into this. Final Bloomsbury thanks to marketing associate Briana Williams, director of publicity Faye Bi, and senior director of education marketing and subrights Beth Eller, I'm grateful you will be helping this book find its way to the readers who need it most.

Every year, my community of fellow children's literature creators keeps expanding, and I am so very grateful for all of you who read, encouraged, re-read, and provided a shoulder to cry on or let me drag them on one of my Hike and Rants. My critique group: Molly Golden, Claire Bobrow, Helen Taylor, Natalie Mitchell, and Joanna Ho. My fire poppies: Andrew Sass, Madeleine Gunhart, A.J. Irving, Tara Hannon, Kristy Everington, Katrina Emmel, Taylor Tracy, and Kara Newhouse. My hummingbirds of hope: Jess Lanan, Shirley Ng-Benitez, Isabella Kung, Kim-Hoa Ung, Meridth Gimbel, Dev Petty, Anne Ursu, and Martha Brockenbrough. All my fellow PB Rising Stars Mentors: but especially Chloe Ito Ward, who promised to come to book launches and cry from the first row so I won't cry alone, and Jerrold Connors because he's a present-day Eric Carle of donuttry who elevates the art to delicious effect and especially because he apparently read (or flipped) this far in the book.

Additional heartfelt thanks to Nikki Grimes for the prayers, the kindness, and the words of strategy and encouragement.

Finally, my family: My parents, mother-in-law, and sister for their continued support and cheerleading. For

Henry and Arthur, you aren't *exactly* Hank and Archie, but there's always something of each of you in all my stories. I am able to write them because of you. And Mark, the takeout, the coffee, the unwavering belief in me: you are always and forever my "lowercase n."